Rumblewick's
MY DIARY

MY Unwilling WITCH
starts a fun park

Hiawyn Oram • Sarah Warburton

ORCHARD BOOKS

KU-520-208

A SHORT HISTORY
OF HOW YOU COME TO BE READING MY
VERY PRIVATE DIARIES

In a snail shell, they were STOLEN. Oh yes, no less. My witch Haggy Aggy (HA for short) sneaked into my log basket and helped herself.

According to her, this is what happened:

On one of her many shopping trips to Your Side she met a Book Wiz. (I am told you call them publishers, though Wiz seems more fitting as they make books appear, as if by magic, every day of the week.)

Anyway, this Book Wiz/publisher wanted HA to write an account of HER life as a witch here on Our Side. Of course, HA wasn't willing to do that. Being the most unwilling witch in witchdom, she is far too busy shopping, watching telly, not cackling, being anything BUT a witch and getting me into trouble with the High Hags* as a result.

The Book Wiz begged on her knees (apparently) and offered HA a life's supply of shoes if she came up with something. So HA did. She came up with THIS — MY DIARIES. ALL OF THEM!!!!

Of course, when I wrote the diaries, I was not expecting anyone to read them. Let alone Othersiders like you. But as you are, here is a word to the wise about how things work between us:

* The High Hags run everything round here. They RULE.

1. We are here on THIS SIDE and you are there on the OTHER SIDE.

2. Between us is the HORIZON LINE.

3. You don't see we're here, on This Side, living our lives, because for you the HORIZON LINE is always a day away. You can walk for a thousand moons (or more for all I know), but you'll never reach it.

4. On the other paw, we know you're there because we visit you all the time. This is partly because of broomsticks. A broomstick has no trouble with any Horizon Line anywhere. A broomstick (with one or more of us upon it) just flies straight through.

And it has to be like that because scaring Otherside children into their wits is part of witches' work. In fact it is Number One on the Witches' Charter of Good Practice (see copy glued at the back).

On the other paw, it is NOWHERE in the Charter for a witch to go over to Your Side to make friends and try to be and do everything you are and do — as my witch Haggy Aggy does.

But then, that's my giant problem: being cat to a witch who doesn't want to be one. And as you will see from these diaries, it makes my life a right BAG OF HEDGEHOGS. So all I can say is, if HA tries to make friends with YOU, send her straight back to This Side with a spider in her ear.

Thank you,

Rumblewick Spellwacker Mortimer B. xxx

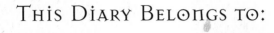

THIS DIARY BELONGS TO:

Rumblewick Spellwacker Mortimer B.

RUMBLEWICK for short, RB for shortest

ADDRESS:
Thirteen Chimneys,
Wizton-under-Wold, This Side
Bird's Eye View: 331 N by WW

TELEPHONE:
77+3-5+1-7

NEAREST OTHERSIDE TELEPHONE:
Ditch and Candleberry Bush Street,
N by SE Over the Horizon

BIRTH DAY:
Windy Day 23rd Magogary

Education:
The Awethunder School For Familiars
12-Moon Apprenticeship to the
High Hag Witch Trixie Fiddlestick

Qualifications:
Certified Witch's Familiar

Current Employment:
Seven-year contract with Witch Hagatha Agatha,
Haggy Aggy for short, HA for shortest

Hobbies:
Catnastics, Point-to-Point Shrewing, Languages

Next of Kin:
Uncle Sherbet (retired Witch's Familiar)
Mouldy Old Cottage,
Flying Teapot Street,
Prancetown

Dear Diary,

Every half moon, all Familiars have to do a turn of duty stacking shelves at the Crafty Witches' Co-Op.

Today was my turn.

I was paired with Witch Rattle's Familiar, Arbuthnot Butnot.

He kept saying he was too tired to open another box of spell ingredients or shake out another cloak — and took naps on the shelves instead of stacking them.

As a result, I did most of the work myself. By the time I staggered back here, I was so worn out I could have fallen asleep standing upright stirring a cauldron.

7

What I did NOT need was what I got: HA exploding like a shooting star with excitement.

Apparently, while I was at the Crafty Co-Op doing community service, she'd gone exploring on the Other Side. And somewhere along the way, she'd discovered the 'Amusement Park'.

"And this, RB," she told me in feverish tones, "is where children go to have fun —

BY SCARING THEMSELVES WITLESS

on gravity-defying contraptions called Roller Coasters and other thrill rides with names like Brainshredder and Dragon Mountain!"

She was so full of the discovery and the experience (she had tried every contraption, of course) she did not stop to draw breath.

"You have to see for yourself," she gab-rabbled.

"I know you'll be completely over the moon. By the upside-downness and looping and steeping and dropping and rolling and swinging and corkscrewing, by the free-falling and total weightlessness and the feeling you'll be spilled and spun into space, any tad of tell, without a broomstick.

It's just HOOTSHOOTERY. MARVELWOCKERY.

And then, RB,
there's the screaming.
It never stops and
herein is my REAL discovery.

Children go on these contraptions to
scream, with terror — yes terror — that is
also pleasure and excitement. And this
means we witches have got it all wrong.
Because, as it turns out,

they LOVE to be scared.
To them, being frightened
is FUN. "

She took a
breath — she
had to or
expire — and
went on.

"So, is this discovery going to change the face of witchdom? Is it going to knock Item No. ⒈ in the Charter of Good Witches' Practice off its perch and into The Blue Beyond All — the Item No. ⒈ that says the primary purpose of witches today is to scare children out of and therefore into their wits? I'll answer my own question for you. *IT IS, IT IS*, because in scaring children we are wasting our time. I've found they are not afraid to be afraid. They're not scared when they're being scared. They're not frightened when their wits are being shredded by that mighty mincing machine called <u>Terror</u>.

Quite the opposite. They can't get enough of it!"

Well, as I said, I was worn out after all the shelf stacking, but when she'd finished — when she'd put it THIS way — I perked right up with my own thrill ride of realisation: Haggy Aggy is exceptional. A one-off. And she's MINE, or rather I am her Familiar — which I hope comes to the same thing.

I know I complain about her. I know I go on. And for good reason. Her unwillingness to be a proper (<u>ordinary</u>) practising witch gets me into one quagmire after another.

But AT THE SAME TAD OF TELL,

if you stop and think about it — which I now did — she is a megalight of marvelwockery. A luminosity in the dark of the everyday. Because, however inconvenient or even dangerous to herself (and me) —

SHE IS ALWAYS
OPEN
TO NEW IDEAS.

And — while obviously I have to keep myself from being hung over a boiling cauldron by the High Hags and/or sent back to first grade for not keeping her in proper practice — I should also be awed and grateful. And serve her dash and dare BETTER.

With this in mind, I have agreed to go with her tomorrow to this Fun Park and experience for myself the phenomenon she believes she has discovered:

THAT CHILDREN LOVE TO BE SCARED.

Dear Diary,

I went — we went. It was outside-of-ordinary and then it got more outside-of-ordinary when HA got carried away and SPELLED ONE OF THE RIDES. It will take some tell to tell you about it — and I will, but, in this case, last things first.

It is not good news. On our way back we had an accident — horribulus to say the least. We'd gone in the car — and were returning in it. HA was driving, gab-rabbling her head off, not looking where she was flying — and we bumped into the High Hags, Dame Amuletta and Trixie Fiddlestick, out for an evening ride on one of their <u>stretch</u> broomsticks.

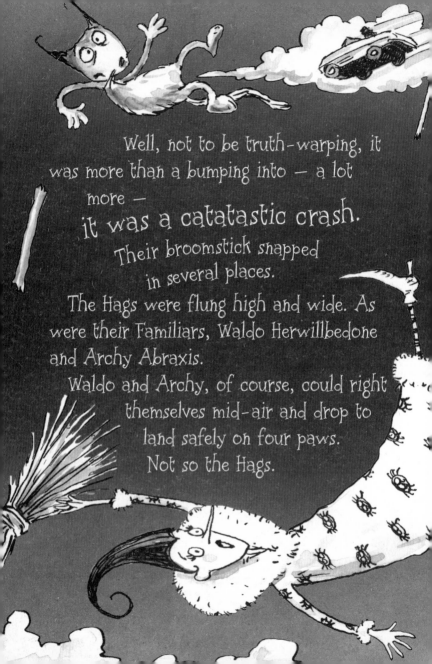

Well, not to be truth-warping, it was more than a bumping into — a lot more —

it was a catatastic crash.

Their broomstick snapped in several places.

The Hags were flung high and wide. As were their Familiars, Waldo Herwillbedone and Archy Abraxis.

Waldo and Archy, of course, could right themselves mid-air and drop to land safely on four paws.

Not so the Hags.

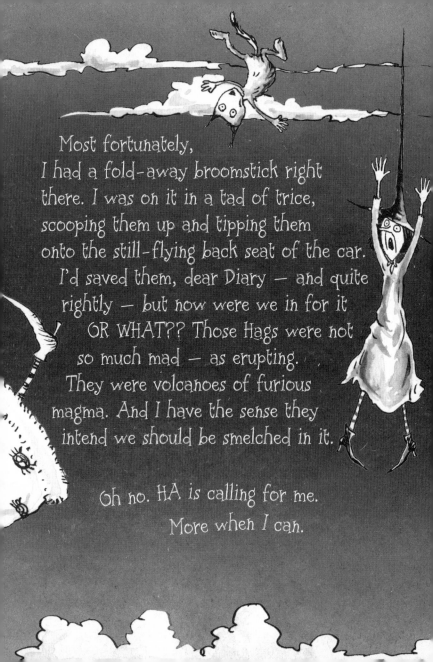

Most fortunately,
I had a fold-away broomstick right
there. I was on it in a tad of trice,
scooping them up and tipping them
onto the still-flying back seat of the car.
I'd saved them, dear Diary — and quite
rightly — but now were we in for it
OR WHAT?? Those Hags were not
so much mad — as erupting.
They were volcanoes of furious
magma. And I have the sense they
intend we should be smelched in it.

Oh no. HA *is* calling for me.
More when I can.

Dear Diary,

Before I go on, I must go back — to my first experience of a Fun Park. It was this in a snail shell: HA is RIGHT and she has made a true discovery:

CHILDREN DO L<u>O</u>VE TO BE SCARED.

In turn, I have made an observation of my own: SO DOES SHE.

While I stood by and watched (or peeped as I couldn't exactly look with both eyes open or I'd stomach launch), she went on every ride and roller coaster — not once or twice but AGAIN and AGAIN. And whose screaming with the pleasure of terror was the loudest? One guess.

Yes. <u>HERS</u>!!!

And THEN, dear Diary, she got bored.

Half way through the day she found me — by this time enjoying the sunset-red fish prize attraction.

(Well, I had to do something while I was doing something else more important which was watching a Grown Othersider who seemed to me to be following us, as if he suspected we might not be what we were trying to pass ourselves off as — ordinary, Fun Park-loving Othersiders!! <u>Why</u>, even now, he was edging up so he could eavesdrop on our conversation.)

"RB," HA cried (not noticing him in her excitement), "these rides are fantabulous but they could be even MORE fantabulous. I've been talking to some children and they agree. So for them, of course, because my primary purpose is to make children cluckhappy, that's what I'm going to do.

I'm going to <u>SPELL</u> a ride into a pleasuredome of terror as yet unscreamed at. Come and see."

And, if you're thinking 'impossible', think again, because that's exactly what she now <u>did</u>!!

She chose a ride called WHIRL ON THE WILD SIDE. In its unspelled state, it was scary enough — a giant wheel contraption inset with two-seater seats round its rim. Once filled with Othersiders — it whirled faster and faster until there was nothing to see but a spinning circle of light.

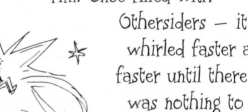

(Or hear but a spinning circle of scream.)

THIS IS THE SPELL SHE USED to send
that Wild Whirl into the furthest reaches
of the terror-pleasure dome:

Whirl on the wild side,
Your whirling is milder
Than the whirling you'll do
Now you're spelled to get wilder
At quite the right moment
With ease and with grace
Your seats will detach
And spin free into space,
Then return once your riders
Have whirled round a star
As the wildest of whirlers
You certainly are!

The spell worked and the commotion
it caused cannot easily be described.

25

The riders — once they'd returned and their seats were re-attached — were white with excitement. When the Wheel stopped, they wouldn't get off. The whole Fun Park resounded with their cries of, "AGAIN!"

All the children who'd seen how came running over screaming,

"OUR TURN!"

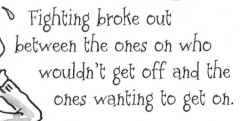

Fighting broke out between the ones on who wouldn't get off and the ones wanting to get on.

Many Grown Othersiders had fallen down in dead faints thinking, perhaps, they'd lost their children to the stars for ever.

Others were on their pocket-sized TVs gab-rabbling to whoever and/or calling for police cellers.

And soon enough, there were police cellers everywhere, filling the Fun Park, closing the rides, separating the fighters, shaking the fainted, questioning 'witnesses' and clearing the Fun Park grounds.

"Oh, RB, what have I done?" HA whispered to me — as we were herded away with the crowd.

"You've changed the nature of Amusement Parks for ever," came a voice — and there he was:

The One
Who I'd Been Watching
Following and
Watching
<u>Us.</u>

He introduced himself as 'Goldtooth, as my friends call me' (and he has a golden tooth, strange as that may be). Then he invited HA for a cup of coffee (the yuk version of comfrey) and

'A LITTLE CHAT'.

Well, this LITTLE CHAT (which I heard from under the table where HA had put me since Goldtooth said he couldn't bear to be too close to a cat) consisted of two parts:

Part 1: he'd been watching her and he'd seen her spelling the Whirl On The Wild Side — <u>hadn't</u> <u>he</u>? It was 'awesome' to behold. She must be a witch. So, was she a witch under her '<u>beautiful</u> <u>exterior</u>'?

(At this HA giggled like the girl she <u>isn't</u> and simpered, "Maybe just a teeny tad of a tadpole of one, though that's still a maybe, <u>not</u> a definite.")

Part ②: well, however little bit of a witch, he went on, you'd never tell from looking. To look at, she was the most entrancing-to-behold woman he'd ever seen. And now he'd seen her, he couldn't let her OUT of his sight. "I am smitten," he swore. "I am yours. I am on my knees to you. Do not cast me into the valley of despond and despair. Say YOU WILL BE MINE. ALL MINE."

I could smell the wet and dry rot of the situation from under the table. But you know Haggy Aggy. Her overflying ambition in the universe is <u>not</u> to be a witch (except when it suits her) but to be beautiful and adored and as Otherside as Othersiders.

She giggled again. "By this do you mean...

will I <u>mar</u>ry you,

Mr Goldtooth?"

"If that's what it takes for you to be mine, all mine, then let us go this minute, and get the ring," he smarmed.

"The ring that shall be rockier than the rocky mountains with precious stones bigger than Peru."

(Didn't know what that meant but no matter.)

33

HA — who knows about Otherside marrying as she often drops in to Otherside libraries to listen to Otherside librarians reading Otherside fairy tales to the children — wasn't letting him off that lightly.

"But are you a <u>prince</u>, Mr Goldtooth?" she asked. "Because, if I'm to marry anyone, he can only be a true and real prince — and not one tiddlytad of a fake who can't feel a pea under nine mattresses."

"Prince?" Goldtooth exploded, as he stood up and called for the coffee account. "Prince? My dear girl, my dear enchantress, forget prince. If you will be mine, I am at once no less than a king. King of the Kingdom of Your Happiness, where your every wish will be my command.

Now come,

let us go purchase

that RING!"

And, in a snail shell, that's why we crashed so catatastrically into the High Hags on their stretch broomstick.

The rocky mountain ring was on HA's spelling finger. She couldn't take her eyes off it — or stop talking about it along with what she was going to wear to her Otherside marry ceremony. She was not looking where she was fly-driving.

Oh no! Someone's here. Sounds like it's Waldo Herwillbedone, Dame Amuletta's Familiar. He's talking to HA. No doubt bringing us A SUMMONS to a High Hags' Hearing to explain crashing into them in a flying pink car and HA wearing everything but her witch's black.

I could soon be smelched in the magma of the Hags' fury, Diary.

So if you never hear another word from me, you'll know <u>why</u>.

Dear Diary,

Waldo <u>had</u> brought a Summons to attend a
High Hags' Hearing.

Needless to say, HA wriggled out of
going.

After Waldo left she said, "Oh RB,
I haven't time. You know what they're like.
Those Hags go on and on about the same
old same old. And I have so much to do
here, thinking about my marry dress and
coming up with ideas for Goldtooth's and
my Fun Park. Because that's what we're
going to do, did I tell you? Start our own
Fun Park — with the Scariest, Scariest,
<u>W</u>ilder Than <u>Wild</u> Side Rides Ever.

It's just all too supernova for words.
We're even going to have a Ghastly Ghoul
Train — with <u>REAL</u> ghosts. I've agreed to
dance on some graves and wake some
actual dead for it! When I told Goldtooth
I could and would, he fell on his knees and
kissed the hem of my dress!"

YIKES AND THRICE YIKES,

SOCKS, SOCKS,

TADPOLES IN SOCKS,

was all
I could
THINK!

When had they decided all this and when had Goldtooth kissed her dress hem? If I'd seen it, I'd have spat in his face. It must have been when they were in the shop buychasing the rocky mountain ring and I was left in the car because he so hates the closeness of 'cats'.

And what was she talking about 'dancing on graves and waking the dead'? This is a witches' practice she considers to be Dark Ages folderol and will normally have nothing to do with!!

Something was VERY wrong here. Even more wrong than usual when she decides to go all Otherside.

Anyway, she didn't attend the Hearing.

I went alone to take the rap. (So what's new?)

When I arrived, Waldo and Archy were already stoking the fire. And the fur-curling chair was already in place, swinging above the steaming cauldron.

Amuletta and Fiddlestick didn't seem to notice or care that HA hadn't come.

They'd already made up
their minds to BLAME ME for
everything — even though it was
me who'd saved them from being
flung far and wide into nowhere.

And blame me they did,
pointing their pointing fingers,
wibbling their chins and
ordering me to 'step into the
chair' and 'learn my lesson'.

Well, you will be glad
to hear, I didn't.
I stood my ground.

I thought on my paws, as it were.

"Your Hagships," I said, "while there is no excuse for Haggy Aggy NOT LOOKING while flying about in her flying car, there is a very good reason WHY she wasn't which I think you will giantly enjoy and therefore overlook all else. That reason is this: she was over-excited because she is going to start a SCARE PARK.

The Scariest Scare Park Ever

where children will have their wits shredded by — in her words — 'that mighty brain-mincing machine called Terror'."

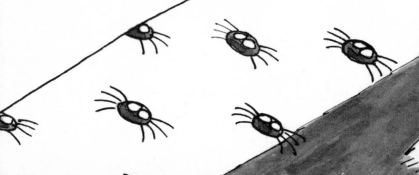

Of course, I left out all the 'fun' bits and Goldtooth and any hint of HA's giant discovery that children LOVE

to be <u>so</u> terrified.

As the Hags' eyes popped  in surprise, I continued:

"So there is no cause for thinking she is not a proper-practising witch or that I am failing in my duties.

She is an EXCEPTIONAL witch." (I did not add <u>when she wants to be</u> but carried straight on.) "Exceptional because she is not only open to new ideas but she HAS new ideas — such as this SCARIEST SCARE PARK FILLED WITH TERROR MACHINES — and she puts her ideas into practice too!" Perfect, brilliant, supernova —

though I say so myself.

The Hags chin-wibbled some more and then waved at Waldo and Archy to stop stoking the fire and take down the fur-curling chair.

They were suddenly all ears and dribbling with greedy interest: when could they come and witness these Mighty Mincing Terror Machines in action?

I told them <u>soon</u>.

I told them I'd let them know.

So here I am, back home from the HH's HQ without so much as one hair on my head curled and feeling pretty pleased with myself.

The only thing is, I can't find HA. She doesn't seem to be here. Maybe she's in the broomstick shed or out feeding the frogs.

I'd better go and see.

Dear Diary,

This is not funny. She is/was not in the shed or feeding the frogs. She wasn't/isn't anywhere...

because she's <u>left</u>.

I mean LEFT 13 CHIMNEYS,

LEFT WIZTON AND THIS SIDE...

LEFT <u>ME</u>...

FOR GOOD!

Here is her note that I found

in my log basket:

51

Dear RB,

I've packed my flying trunk and I've gone — to the Other Side to marry King Goldtooth and start our Scariest Fun Park Ever. I am HIS now, all his. And I will not be back. Not ever.

Do not think I would not prefer it if you could come with me. I would but you can't. Goldie will not have it. He has an aversion to cats. And besides he has two giant dogs who, he says, "would soon make mince meat of you."

I shall miss you, RB, not least because you are the most faithful, resourceful, inventive Familiar a witch could ever have.

(Mind you that's another reason why you cannot come with me. Othersiders do not have Familiars and I'm going to be all Otherside now.)

I have taken the car not a broomstick — and you can have them all. I am sure they will come in handy when you are in service to another witch. She will never be as fantabulous as me but she may be more willing. And you may have an easier time of it.

I can only wish you a supernova future as I'm sure you wish me one.

Yours, NO LONGER A WITCH —

OR HARDLY AT ALL,

HA xx

I'm crushed, dear Diary. Thank the stars I have you because WHAT NOW? What am I going to do?

Instincts are there to be trusted. So that's what I'll do. I'll trust mine. As I said, I smelt the dry and the wet rot about 'King Goldtooth' from the start. The way he crept round the Fun Park, watching her. The way he spoke to her about the Kingdom of Her Happiness — greasy as clove oil. He's after something, Diary. Something slimy and sulphurous.

Something BOG ROTTEN. I can feel it.

And now I think about it, it doesn't take broomstick science to work out WHAT:

he's after her witchcraft.

It has to be. He sensed we weren't any old Othersiders from the moment he set eyes on us and started watching HA carefully — and was watching her when she spelled that Whirling Wheel. He saw her powers. AND NOW HE WANTS TO HARNESS THEM FOR HIMSELF!!

So, if I'm right and I'm sure I am, there's not a tad of tell to lose. I must be after her, find her and STOP HIM. Before he uses her for his own rotten ends.

Dear Diary,

I am writing this by the light of
the moon — lying low in an
outhouse in Goldtooth's
garden which is filled with
broken pieces from Fun Park
rides. It is late — so late it
will soon be dawning.

I packed my satchel, the moment I put
down my pen to you, and came to rescue
Haggy Aggy. But where was I to find her?
At that point, I had no address — no
notion of where Goldtooth lived.

I hovered around the entrance to the Fun
Park until it closed — in the hope that she
and Goldtooth would arrive.

They didn't. So, using my highly-developed sense of smell, I retraced my own pawsteps from when the three of us left the Fun Park and went to the coffee rooms — and from there to where we'd parked HA's car. Taking my life in my hands and nearly getting run over several times I followed the scent of our wheels — quite different to the smell of Otherside car wheels — all the way to the Ring Shop. It was locked up tight as an unripe hazel nut. But I squeezed in through a hole billowing hot air in a back wall.

As soon as I was inside, bells started shrilling and soon I could hear police celler sirens advancing.

I don't like that sound — it makes me lose my wits and want to wail at the moon — but in the interest of finding Haggy Aggy, I made myself KEEP them and set about sniffing for the scent of Goldtooth.

And suddenly, there it was — a distinct whiff of him on a piece of paper in a cupboard under the counter.

I breathed it in deep, stuffed the paper into my satchel — and fled the Shop the way I'd come in.

Outside, I easily picked up his scent on the footpath and followed it here.

And, though there is no sign of HA so far, I've peered in a downstairs window and seen him sitting at the kitchen table with a woman Othersider. There were two giant dogs at their feet who sat up and growled — NO DOUBT PICKING UP MY SCENT!

So far, I have not been able to see more or go in.

All the other curtains are closed and all the windows shut.

That's why I'm here in this outhouse — waiting till morning when,

with a bit of luck,

a window or door

is sure to be left open.

Dear Diary,

Even though I am back home snug in my log basket, my paw shakes at the thought of what happened the next day:

A window <u>was</u> opened — on an upper floor.

I squeezed in with my satchel and went in search of HA. And how right I was when I said Goldtooth was all wrong.

I soon found her...

> not by seeing her but
> by <u>hearing</u> her moaning and groaning.

GOLDTOOTH HAD HER LOCKED UP

IN HER OWN FLYING TRUNK!!

When I'd recovered from the shock,
I rapped on the trunk.

She moaned, "Water. Bring me water, you evil witch-nappers."

I rapped again and whispered as loud as I dared, "Haggy Aggy, it's me, RB. What's going on. How did you get in there?"

There was silence for a tad of tell. Then she suppressed a sob and whispered.

"Oh RB. If only you knew.

How I've been tricked."

I told her to have courage while
I unlocked the trunk.

But, before I could work out how to
open the lock, there was a blast of
ferocious growling — and the two giant
dogs I'd seen in the kitchen came hurling
themselves up the stairs and into the room.

In a trice,
I was back out the window,
snatching up
my satchel.

From the ledge outside,
   I leapt onto the roof — the
            dogs biting
               at my heels.

They weren't able to follow me onto the roof so there, heart pounding, I made myself small behind a chimney and — somehow, in spite of the jellied state I was in — spelled myself SCENT FREE, inventing the spell right there on the spot!

Of course, I wouldn't know if it had worked until it was put to the test. But, hopeful that I could now pass by those dogs without them sniffing my presence, I made myself invisible as well (using our Tried and Tested Out of Sighter).

Next, I hid my precious satchel

in the chimney stack and

re-entered the house.

To my relief, both spells had worked. To my distress I found:

[1] Goldtooth and the woman Othersider — sitting together on a sofa — nibbling each others' ears. He called her 'Silver Sweetheart' or 'Silverstuds' (she was studded all over with silver bits). "We're going to be rich," he whispered. "Very rich. We're going to be millwinaires. And all because I had the savvy to win over a witch when I saw one."

② Silverstuds — <u>who was wearing</u> <u>HA's rocky ring</u>, said, "And because I had the savvy to lock her up in her own trunk having fed her my special brew of root soup so laced with Drowsadin she doesn't know her foot from her elbow and can't use her own magic to escape!"

<u>YIKES</u>, <u>THRICE YIKES</u> and <u>HELP</u> kept going through my mind. Drowsadin??? It must be some kind of powerful Otherside potion.

This was a disaster and then it got worse.

They decided it was time to take HA 'out for a little amusement'.

I followed them — invisible and unsniffed — as they went upstairs and opened the trunk. When HA sat up and stretched, Silverstuds force fed her some small blue lozenges.

"To give you back your strength, my dear, come along, eat up your nice sweeties," she sneered.

I watched in horror as HA swallowed and immediately started obeying their orders.

The first of these was to come with them and get in their car.

At this,
I raced back
to the roof and
my satchel, spelled
myself visible again (I can't fly a
broomstick invisible), got out my foldaway
and flew along following their car.

And soon the dark depths of Goldtooth
and Silverstuds' evil designs for using HA
for their own rotten ends were made plain.

They took her to a Fun Park — well,
a Fun Park of sorts. It was theirs — and it
wasn't fun. It wasn't even open. There were
no excited children queuing for
their terror thrills. Rides were
broken. Paintwork was peeling.
Sunset-red fish bowls were empty
of everything except rain water.
A carriage of what had
once been a Ghost Train
                lay on its side.

Keeping well out of sight as I flew down, I crept into the carriage, from there to observe the goings on.

"And now," I heard Goldtooth say to HA, "if you don't want to spend the rest of your life locked in your own trunk, start spelling. Make these rides the most terrifyingly thrilling ever or be sorry."

How the
shivers attacked
me as I saw my
witch walking round
like she'd just been roused from
the dead. And — worst of all — so

MEEKLY OBEYING the horribulus

Goldtooth and the trunk-locking,

potion-feeding Silverstuds!

As if in a trance, she approached
a Big Wheel that was rusting and
leaning on its side. She raised her
spelling finger and started to
chant in a lifeless voice.

And this is when something in me
SNAPPED.
I drew in a great gulp of air — air inspires
me — streaked across the grass and
(inventing on the spot) turned Goldtooth
and Silverstuds into TWO SUNSET-RED FISH
SWIMMING ROUND IN ONE
RAINWATER-FILLED
BOWL!

Then I picked up the rocky ring that had somehow flown off Silverstuds' finger during the spell and landed in the grass — and went over to Haggy Aggy.

She was so drowsadinned and/or otherwise tranced, she hadn't noticed what I'd done. She was still pointing and numbly chanting at the Big Wheel.

I interrupted and <u>MADE</u> her look at me.

She shook herself and blinked, staring without seeing or as if she didn't know who I was. And then slowly she began to focus and come out of her daze.

"Rumblewick!" she said softly. "Where are we? Where have you brought me? I'm cold and hungry. Shall we go home? Have you a broomstick?

Of course you have.

You're never without one of <u>those</u>!"

76

I'll go on later — right now I must go
and check on HA who I can hear groaning
and calling, no doubt from the
middle of a nightsnake
about those <u>evil</u> witchnappers
and being locked
in her own
flying trunk!

Dear Diary,

Been VERY busy since I last wrote but now have some time to finish the Fun Park saga.

And it <u>has</u> ended well, dear Diary. So well, I couldn't be more pleased.

Once I'd got HA to focus and shown her the fish in the bowl — and we'd both admired my spelling work — I flew us home.

Here I got her warm on the sofa and cheffed up her favourite Ragwort Hot Pot with Pine Needle Salad.

Then I showed her the note she'd left me before 'going to the Other Side <u>for ever</u> to marry King Goldtooth'.

This jogged her back to life, I can tell you.

Now everything came back to her. She tried to be furious with Goldtooth — and so did I — but when we thought of him swimming round with Silverstuds in a small bowl of murky rainwater, for the rest of their lives, we couldn't help but laugh.

And the laughter did her much good.

She was soon her old bubbling-over self and having one of her impossible IDEAS.

"RB," she said, "that broken down old Fun Park. It's nobody's now. It's just sitting there, rubbling to bits.

So why don't we turn it into <u>MY</u> SCARIEST SCARY FUN PARK EVER ?

We'll not only make a lot of children very happy, we'll make <u>me</u> over the moon — because I'll be able to

GO ON ALL THE RIDES, ANY TIME I LIKE!"

Well, I'll not truth-warp here, Diary. Normally I would have done everything to put her off the idea. As a proper-practising witch, I knew she should not be thinking of taking thrilling rides in a Fun Park on the Other Side. Or of making a lot of children very happy.

But — and it's a giant but — I still had the spectre of Dame Amuletta and Trixie Fiddlestick waiting

impatiently to witness HA's Terror Machines in <u>action</u>!

So I did NOT put her off the idea.
                    I ENCOURAGED it.
And offered some practical help.

"Very well," I said, "but remember what happened when you spelled that Whirl On The Wild Side contraption. The Growns called the Police Cellers who closed the Park down!"

"Good thinking, RB," she said and then, in a tad of trice, came up with

a brilliant solution.

It was this:

TO SPELL

AN ENCHANTED CIRCLE

AROUND HER SCARY FUN PARK

THAT MADE IT <u>INVISIBLE</u> TO GROWN

OTHERSIDERS.

AN ENCHANTED CIRCLE THROUGH WHICH

ONLY CHILDREN COULD PASS!!

And that is just what she has done.
For now, EVERYONE is happy.
Children can enter the Fun Park and
enjoy such fantabulous rides as:

the Supernova Screamer

the Leave The Earth Coaster

the Slippery Slope to No-town

the Caverns of the Freshly Woken Dead

and, of course,

the Whirl to the Wild Side of Space.

Their Growns —
completely unaware
of what their children
are enjoying — are in ignorant bliss.

The Hags, who came by this morning,
disguised as fluffy pink prize rabbits (we
insisted), heard the screams of terror,
didn't understand the terror was pleasure
and ALL IN FUN — and are

MOST
<u>FAVOURABLY</u>
IMPRESSED.

(And I'm out
of the Blame
Chair for now.)

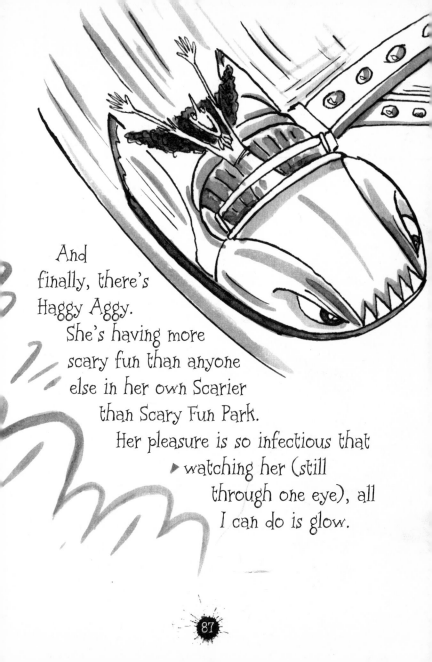

And
finally, there's
Haggy Aggy.
She's having more
scary fun than anyone
else in her own Scarier
than Scary Fun Park.
Her pleasure is so infectious that
▶ watching her (still
through one eye), all
I can do is glow.

Of course, I'm also hoping she will do what she usually does when she throws herself helter-skelter into some new aspect of Otherside life...

which is GET BORED SOON.

Mind you, one thing's for sure. I will <u>never</u> get bored watching a certain two sunset-red fish swimming round — and round and round — in a Fun Park bowl!

Well, that's it for now, dear Diary. I'm off to bring HA's flying trunk home — from that evil witchnapper's house. Which reminds me. I've still got the rocky mountain ring with its Peru-sized precious stones in my satchel.
I wonder what I should do with it. Any ideas, let me know.

PS: Wish you _could_ speak to me.

Imagine:
'Rumblewick Spellwacker
    Mortimer B
        and his
Talking Diary!'

Would that be a wondrous thing,
    or what?

SPELL TO TURN TWO TRICKSOME WITCHNAPPERS INTO LITTLE RED SWIMMERS

(As invented on the spur of necessity
by Rumblewick Spellwacker Mortimer B)

Come sunset red
Come gills and scales
Come four pop eyes
Come two fin tails
Oh you who nabbed
And tricked and stole
ARE TWO COLD FISH
IN A VERY SMALL BOWL!

SPELL TO MAKE YOURSELF UNSNIFFABLE

Wrap tail round self, tuck in ears, curl up into small ball and chant:

I cannot be detected
By anybody's snout
The keenest nose existing
Will never find me out
There's nothing me that's sniffable
There's nothing me that's whiffable
My perfume's unlocatable
My whereabouts unstatable
I haven't got an odour
A whiff, a tang or scent
For when it comes to body smell
It suddenly JUST WENT!

By the way, here are the
spells I've mentioned!
Enjoy.

THE TRIED-AND-TRUSTED-OUT-OF-SIGHT SPELL

Make a breeze by sneezing seven times.
Curl your Lucky Whisker backwards and chant:

It's in your own interest
That you're out of sight
So wherever you are
There is nothing but light,
Not an arm or a thumb
Not a leg or a tum
Not one scrap or one cell
Though you're perfectly well
Not a hair in between
When this spell is said
CAN BE SEEN!

WITCHES' CHARTER
OF GOOD PRACTICE

1. Scare at least one child on the Other Side
into his or her wits – every day (excellent),
once in seven days (good), once a moon (average),
once in two moons (bad), once in a blue
moon (failed).

2. Identify any fully-grown Othersiders who
were not properly scared into their wits as
children and DO IT NOW. (It is never too
late for a grown Othersider to come to
his or her senses.)

3. Invent a new spell useful for every purpose and
every occasion in the Witches' Calendar.
Ensure you or your Familiar commits it to
a Spell Book before it is lost to the
Realms of Forgetfulness for ever.

4. Keep a proper witch's house at all
times – filled with dust and spiders' webs, mould
and earwigs underthings and ensure the jars on
your kitchen shelves are always alive with
good spell ingredients.

5. Cackle a lot. Cackling can be heard far and wide and serves many purposes such as (i) alerting others to your terrifying presence (ii) sounding hideous and thereby comforting to your fellow witches.

6. Make sure your Familiar keeps your means of proper travel (broomsticks) in good trim and that one, either or both of you exercise them regularly.

7. Never fail to present yourself anywhere and everywhere in full witch's uniform (i.e. black everything and no ribbons upon your hat ever). Sleeping in uniform is recommended as a means of saving dressing time.

8. Keep your Familiar happy with a good supply of Comfrey and Slime Buns. Remember, behind every great witch is a well-fed Familiar.

9. At all times acknowledge the authority of your local High Hags. As their eyes can do 360 degrees and they know everything there is to know, it is always in your interests to make their wishes your commands.

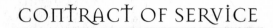

CONTRACT OF SERVICE

between
WITCH HAGATHA AGATHA, Haggy Aggy for short, HA for shortest
of Thirteen Chimneys, Wizton-under-Wold

&

the Witch's Familiar,
RUMBLEWICK SPELLWACKER MORTIMER B, RB for short

It is hereby agreed that, come
FIRE, Brimstone, CAULDRONS overflowing
or ALIEN WIZARDS invading,
for the NEXT SEVEN YEARS
RB will serve HA,
obey her EVERY WHIM AND WORD and at all times assist her
in the ways of being a true and proper WITCH.

PAYMENT for services will be:
* a log basket to sleep in   * unlimited Slime Buns for breakfast
* free use of HA's broomsticks (outside of peak brooming hours)
* and a cracked mirror for luck.

PENALTY for failing in his duties will be decided on the whim of
THE HAGS ON HIGH.

SIGNED AND SEALED
this New Moon Day, 22nd of Remember

Haggy Aggy
....
Witch Hagatha Agatha

Rumblewick
....
Rumblewick Spellwacker Mortimer B

Trixie Fiddlestick
....
And witnessed by the High Hag, Trixie Fiddlestick

ORCHARD BOOKS

338 Euston Road, London NW1 3BH
Orchard Books Australia
Level 17/207 Kent Street, Sydney NSW 2000

ISBN: 978 1 84616 071 4

First published in 2008 by Orchard Books

Text © Hiawyn Oram 2008
Cover illustrations © Sarah Warburton 2008
Inside illustrations © Orchard Books 2008

A CIP catalogue record for this book is

available from the British Library.

Orchard Books is a division
of Hachette Children's Books

1 3 5 7 9 10 8 6 4 2
Printed in China/Hong Kong

To my sister — our
megalight of marvelwockery
H.O.

For Joseph
S.W.

Dear Precious Children

The Publisher asked me to say something about these Diaries.
(As I do not write Otherside very well, I have dictated it to
the Publisher's Familiar/assistant. If she has not written it
down right, let me know and I'll turn her into a fat pumpkin.)

This is my message: I went to a lot of trouble to steal these
Diaries for you. And the Publisher gave me a lot of shoes in
exchange. If you do not read them the Publisher may want the
shoes back. So please, for my sake — the only witch in
witchdom who isn't willing to scare you for her own
entertainment — ENJOY THEM ALL.
Yours ever,

Haggy Aggy

Your fantabulous shoe-loving friend,
Hagatha Agatha (Haggy Aggy for short, HA for shortest) xx

ISBN 9781846160653

ISBN 9781846160691

ISBN 9781846160721

ISBN 9781846160714

ISBN 9781846160677

ISBN 9781846160660

ISBN 9781846160707

ISBN 9781846160684